Ghost on Board

Gettysburg Ghost Gang # 2

By

Shelley Sykes

and

Lois Szymanski

WHITE MANE KIDS
SHIPPENSBURG, PENNSYLVANIA

This White Mane Books publication
was printed by
Beidel Printing House, Inc.
63 West Burd Street
Shippensburg, PA 17257-0152 USA

The acid-free paper used in this book meets the guidelines for permanence and durability of the Committee on Production Guidelines for Book Longevity of the Council on Library Resources.

For a complete list of available publications
please write
White Mane Books
Division of White Mane Publishing Company, Inc.
P.O. Box 152
Shippensburg, PA 17257-0152 USA

Library of Congress Cataloging-in-Publication Data

Sykes, Shelley.
    Ghost on board / by Shelley Sykes and Lois Szymanski.
        p. cm. -- (Gettysburg ghost gang ; #2)
    Summary: Three young boys rely on the help of their ghost-friend, Corporal Jared Scott, to solve the mystery of a new ghost that appears at Cavalry Ridge Campground.
    ISBN 1-57249-267-8
    [1. Ghosts--Fiction. 2. Camps--Fiction. 3. Recreational vehicles--Fiction. 4. Gettysburg (Pa.)--Fiction.] I. Szymanski, Lois. II. Title.

PZ7.S9834 Gh 2001
[Fic]--dc21
                                                                    2001026503

PRINTED IN THE UNITED STATES OF AMERICA

To the boys and girls of the Carroll Writer's Guild. Barry, Scott, Becky, Sue, Terri and Julie who guide our spirits through the writing process.

————————————

Both authors are grateful to Mark Nesbitt for allowing them to put him face to face, fictionally, with a ghost.

Contents

Chapter One
The Jamboree

Philip, his younger brother Zach, who held the flashlight, and their friend Chucky strolled along the winding campground road. The night air stirred as a cool breeze wrapped them in the lingering smell of wood fires and sweet toasted marshmallows.

Zach swept the flashlight beam in a wide arch. "Looks like everybody that wanted to go to the campfire has already gone."

"Dad worries that someone might miss out on the fun if they didn't see the sign." Philip nudged his glasses higher on his nose and slowed his walk. The biweekly jamboree in the center grounds meant a lot to his father. It was something that he felt set Cavalry Ridge Campground apart from the others.

"Hey," Chucky said. His feet crunched on the gravel as he came to a stop. "What's that banging?"

Philip and Zach swung their heads to catch where the sound was coming from. A thumping noise just around the bend sounded like someone was hitting a picnic table with a metal pan.

"Somebody's cleaning up from supper," Zach said.

Chucky shrugged and jiggled a mess of unknown objects in his pockets. The clatter almost drowned out the other. As the boys neared the bend Zach swung the flashlight toward the noise.

Just then, an elderly man's voice yelled, "Stop it! Just stop it!"

The boys halted in their tracks as the flashlight beam fell on Mr. Creach. The old gentleman sat at the splintered table, his hands over his ears and his head shaking back and forth. The noise had stopped.

Philip remembered Mr. Creach from that morning when he had pulled into the campground and asked for a site away from the others. The recreational vehicle he towed behind his station wagon was rusted in spots where the pea green paint had flaked off.

Philip took the flashlight from Zach and started toward the man. "Mr. Creach? Are you okay, sir?"

"What?" The old man looked at Philip in surprise, squinting at the light. "Who is that?"

"It's Philip Baxter, Mr. Creach. We heard somebody yell."

Mr. Creach slid his legs out from under the table and stood up. "I didn't hear any yelling," he said.

The boys looked at each other.

"Are you coming to the jamboree?" Chucky asked.

"What's that?" Mr. Creach looked puzzled.

"Just a bunch of folks," Chucky said, reciting the sign that was posted at the office, from memory, "a little music, and a little fun, with mountain pies and funnel cakes, under a starry sky."

Zach stifled a laugh and Philip elbowed him. There was something not quite right nagging Philip. He shrugged off the feeling.

"Other folks around, huh?"

"Sure! Lot's of folks, Mr. Creach."

"Maybe I'll go at that."

Chucky seemed overly happy about the convincing he'd done. "Just stay on the lane. You'll hear the music and you can follow the sound."

Without a backward glance Mr. Creach stepped past them and started up the road.

"That guy's weird," Zach whispered.

"He's probably shy," Chucky countered.

"I don't know, Chucky," Philip said. He looked around the campsite. He noticed the nagging feeling again. "Something is weird all right but whether it's Mr. Creach or not, I don't know." He played the light over the campsite. "Does anyone see any camping gear?"

"Not unless you count the RV," Zach snorted.

"Hey!" Chucky said. "Philip's right. There's no fire, no lantern on the table, no coolers. Even people with RVs have coolers sitting around. There's just the car. And what _was_ that banging noise we heard?"

"Whatever it was, Mr. Creach was the one yelling for it to stop," Philip answered. A finger of cold inched up his spine. He shook it away. "Let's get out of here."

* * * * *

There was a good turnout at the jamboree. Gloria Coppersmith, Chucky's mom, was twirling batter from a funnel into two large cast iron skillets filled with hot oil. She set that batter down and adjusted the flame on the camp stove burners.

"You guys want a funnel cake?" she offered. "It's on the house."

Chucky hitched up his pants. "Thanks, Mom."

"Thanks," Philip added. "Where's my dad?"

"He's still manning the mountain pies," Gloria said, pointing toward the large bonfire in midfield. "He gets all the volunteers," she complained.

It seemed like Mr. Baxter was never short of helpers to make mountain pies. There was something appealing about making a sandwich from bread and pie filling. They sprinkled it with sugar, then clamped it shut in the pie iron, and shoved it into the embers at the edge of the fire.

Philip counted three men near his dad at a table away from the fire's harshest heat. Two men were loading the iron pie forms while his dad was retrieving one by its three-foot long handle. The other man was watching the pie makers. Philip recognized him in the soft glow that didn't come entirely from the fire.

"Hey, let's go say hi to Dad," he suggested.

"Here, take a funnel cake," Gloria said, "and if you see Casey send her over."

"You want me to help, Mom?" Chucky sprinkled powdered sugar onto the funnel cake and pulled it apart into three portions.

Zach bit into his right away, disregarding how hot it was.

Philip cautiously blew on his. They all loved the sweet spider web-shaped cakes. They tasted like donuts, but lighter and crispier on the outside.

"No, you go ahead," Gloria said. "Just send your sister along. I'm going to keep these few warm and only make more if someone asks."

As they walked toward Mr. Baxter, Chucky and Zach saw the man standing near him too. They both laughed and broke into a trot.

"Hey, Dad!"

"Hi, boys."

"Everybody's here tonight," Philip said. "We even got Mr. Creach to come. Have you seen him?"

"Yeah, I did. I think he went over to the band."

A country band was playing music on a flatbed wagon at the far end of the field. People sat in lawn chairs and on blankets listening, and some were dancing.

Mr. Baxter introduced the men helping him. "This is Jim Hoffman from Philadelphia, and Bob Stewart from Minnesota. These are my boys, Philip and Zach, and their friend Chucky."

None of the boys found it odd that the third man was left out of the introductions, because they were the only ones who knew he was there. Corporal Jared Scott, their friend and resident Civil War ghost, smiled and nodded too. A soft bluish glow surrounded him.

"I knew they were Yankees," he said, and the boys laughed quietly.

It always amazed the boys that Jared could walk with them and among other people and never be seen or heard. He was so real to them, just as real as anyone else in the campground was and there were times they'd gotten funny looks for talking "to themselves."

Seeing Jared now, Philip wondered about the strange feeling that he'd had at Mr. Creach's campsite. He remembered the cold, like a finger on his spine and how it had been almost the same when he had first encountered the corporal. There was definitely something wrong at that campsite.

A song ended and Mr. Baxter took the opportunity to raise a bullhorn to his mouth. "Don't forget mountain pies and funnel cakes! Come and place your orders!"

Several people made their way to the table and Gloria shouted that she had funnel cakes.

"Come on you guys," Philip said. Chucky, Zach and Jared followed him to the other side of the fire and sat down around him on the warm ground. The grass tickled the undersides of Philip's legs and he scratched them.

"What's up, Jared?" Zach asked as he lay on his back to watch the stars.

"Like you guys always say: 'Same old, same old.'"

They laughed with him.

"I was watching that campsite you told me about. The one where the two guys are staying."

"The reenactors?" Zach asked. The boys knew Jared was interested in the people who dressed in uniforms and reenacted the battles and encampments from the Civil War, and made sure to tell him if any were staying with them.

"They have the cleanest uniforms I've seen. It's a little strange to see. I wish I could talk to them sometimes."

"Do you wish you could taste one of those pies, Corporal?" Chucky insisted on calling Jared by his proper rank, no matter how many times Jared told him he didn't have to. Chucky was keen on soldiers, whatever war they had been in, and it was just his way.

Jared shrugged. "I never thought about it. If I wanted to eat, I could find some fellows to eat with." He waved his hand in the vicinity of the woods and Philip couldn't help the shiver that ran over him.

Jared had told them that there were other spirits about the campground. He wasn't the only one. But he was the only one that Philip and the others cared to see. It was nice to sit and talk to Jared, not to be worried about people noticing the way they grouped together with a space big enough for another person in their circle.

Philip listened to the chatter and looked around. Then he saw Mr. Creach. The old man was walking away from the band and toward them. He stepped quickly, head down, and was almost on them when Philip scrunched out of the way.

"Hey," he yelled as Mr. Creach's leg went right through Jared Scott, who didn't seem to feel a thing.

But Mr. Creach must have felt something. The old man froze and looked around, the gaze from his craggy face landing on each boy for a second. "Who did I step on?" he asked.

"No one," Philip said.

Mr. Creach put out a hand and waved it from side to side, like a blind person feeling for an obstacle. The hand went through Jared's head and the soldier stood up.

"Cold!" Mr. Creach hissed and backed up a step. "I…it's following me now!"

Before the boys could react, Mr. Creach was running at a pretty good pace toward the road.

"What is he talking about?" The corporal looked stunned. "I haven't been following him."

Philip looked around and shivered. "Then what has?"

Chapter Two
Checking on Mr. Creach

"Was it something I said?" Chucky shrugged his shoulders, looking bewildered despite his attempt to joke. Mr. Creach was already out of sight.

"Did you take a bath today?" Zach teased his friend with a grin.

Philip elbowed his brother. "This isn't funny, Zach. Something is really wrong with that guy. I had a feeling about it when we were at his campsite, but now I know it's true."

Chucky sank his hands deep into his pockets, nervously juggling his collection of junk. "You don't think he saw Corporal Scott, do you?"

Jared straightened. "Certainly not. No one else does, so why should he?"

Philip wrinkled his brow in thought before answering Jared. "The only ones who have ever been able to see you are those who have handled the I.D. tag we found when we dug you up."

Jared shook his head. "You did not *dig me up,*" he said indignantly.

Philip started to tap Jared's arm and felt a tingle as his fingers passed through. "You know what I mean," he said apologetically. "No one could see you until we dug up your I.D. tag. Then we saw you. Mark Nesbitt saw you after he touched it too," Philip said, reminding him of the local writer who collected ghost stories from Gettysburg. He'd come to help the boys and had seen Jared himself.

"I don't care what you say," Zach said. "I'd say that old guy knew Jared was there. Did you see how he felt around in the air? Then he got that wild-eyed look, like a deer zapped by headlights!" He got up from the ground and began to pace. "What are we going to do if he tells someone?"

"Sit back down, Zach, you're making me nervous," Philip said. "Something's not right, but I don't think it's because of Jared. Remember what he said? He said, 'It's following me now.' Like he'd run into *it* before, whatever *it* is, and I don't think he meant Jared."

Everyone was silent for a moment, except for Chucky jingling the stuff in his pockets. Across the way a few campers made their way down the hill toward their campsite. The jamboree was starting to break up. Applause for the country band drifted over them like the smoke that rose from the dying campfire. Chucky could see his mom and Don Baxter packing up their equipment. Their heads bent together and they talked in low tones.

"Life's a mystery, boys," Jared said softly. "Some things you just have to let rest."

Zach went to the fire and plucked a stick from it. With its glowing red tip he wrote circles in the air. "What you said, Jared, that might be true," he said with a sigh. "But I'm going to keep my eye on Mr. Creach just the same."

* * * * *

Zach's plans for the week included purposely walking past Mr. Creach's campsite at least once a day, and he made sure Philip and Chucky came along. On Tuesday Jared had come along.

By Thursday Philip was beginning to worry.

"It's quiet all right," he said as the three settled on the picnic table at the site next to the old RV. "But it's too quiet!"

Chucky turned his ball cap on his head. "What do you mean?" he asked. "Nothing's going on here. That's good."

"No it's not."

Zach snorted. "Of course it is. Nothing happening is good. Nothing happening is safe. I like safe."

"Is it?"

Zach elbowed Philip. "Knock it off, Philip, and spill your guts. Tell us what you're talking about."

Philip pulled a ring of keys up from his belt. They were the keys to the soda machines in the campground. "Let's take a walk and get a soda," he suggested.

As they walked Philip began to talk. "It *has* been quiet," he admitted. "But I haven't seen Mr. Creach in a while. Have you?"

Zach and Chucky both shook their heads, falling into step beside Philip.

"That might not be good," Philip said. "I mean…if something was following him…if something was after him…well, what if something *was* after him? Where is Mr. Creach now?"

Zach's eyes widened. Then silence hung between them as each boy thought of the possibilities.

At the soda machine, Philip put a key in the door and turned it, then he swung the door wide. Each boy reached to choose a soda. Philip pulled a note pad from his pocket and jotted down how much money they owed the machine.

As they popped the tabs and sipped away the fizz, Zach finally said what they were each thinking. "What if it got him? Whatever it is?"

Chucky sat down on a bench, sitting his soda beside him. He rooted in his pockets and pulled out a quarter, which he handed to Philip. "Here," he said. "Add this to what I owe the machine."

Next he pulled a yo-yo from his pocket. "Gee," he said, "I don't even want to think about what it is…or where Mr. Creach is." He released the yo-yo and it rolled down the string and back up again.

"I think we should go back to the trailer and check on him," Philip said.

Zach rolled his eyes. "We've been checking on him all week."

"No we haven't," Philip said, marking the quarter down in his note pad. "We've spied on his site but we haven't seen him, so we haven't checked on him."

Zach looked irritated, but Chucky seemed puzzled. He rolled up the yo-yo and put it back in his pocket. "What's the difference? What can we do?"

Philip looked at him. "I think we should knock on the door and make sure that he is all right."

Zach leaned against the soda machine. "I don't want to do that. You know the old guy's weird!"

"Do you have a better idea?" Philip asked.

"Yeah, I say we just forget it. Forget what we saw, and forget about the old man and how he acted the other night."

"I don't get it," Philip said. "You're the one who made us check on the site every evening this week!"

Zach put his soda can to his forehead, moving it across and back. "Well, I was wrong!"

Chucky could feel a fight coming on and he didn't want to be in the middle of it. "Come on, guys, don't argue. What can it hurt to check? We knock on the door and if he answers we just tell him about Friday night, when the reenactors are going to be camped at the field. We'll act like we're going around letting all the campers know, just like we did for the jamboree."

"And if he's not there?"

Before Chucky could answer, Philip took charge. "Like Dad always says, we'll cross that bridge when we come to it."

"If we come to it," Chucky pitched in.

"Let's do it then," Philip said.

"Right n-n-now?" Zach asked. He blew upwards, his bangs flying up from his forehead with the force of his breath.

"Of course, now!"

They walked without talking. Philip led them at a fast clip down the path they had worn thin all week. In no time at all they were standing outside the circle of Mr. Creach's site again, staring at the pea green recreational vehicle.

"Well, go ahead," Zach dared Philip. "It was your idea. We'll wait here."

The pattern of rusty spots that Philip was looking at seemed to wind around the camper like a serpent. It etched itself into Philip's mind, like an evil sign. No breeze stirred the summer air, but a chill crept over him, just the same.

"Go on," Zach said again. "You're the brave one."

Philip spun around. "Shut up!" He walked toward the trailer, stepped gingerly up the metal steps and knocked three times on the door.

Zach and Chucky stood in the shadows, watching, and waiting but no one answered the door.

Philip rapped again, even louder, then once more. He turned to face the shadows and gestured palms up. A moment later he hopped off the steps. "I don't think he's here."

Chucky stepped forward. "I hope he's okay," he said with hesitation.

Philip's back was to the trailer when he felt a cool shroud of air rise and wrap itself around him, like a boa constrictor. He shook away the chill and turned to see if the others felt it too. But before he could read their faces, his eyes widened and he jumped as a clatter arose from inside the camper.

All three boys backed into the next site, their mouths open with fear. The volume of the clatter rose and as it did the trailer began to rock, as if it were being whipped by high winds. But not even a breeze stirred.

Zach's fingers bit into Chucky's arm. Chucky had backed into Philip, who was speechless. All three boys watched as the trailer rocked, and banged, and moaned.

Chapter Three
The Eerie RV

"What the heck is gong on?" Zach yelled. "Is it an earthquake?"

"In Gettysburg?" Philip tried to remain calm.

"It's gotta be Mr. Creach in there," Chucky said.

"It's not." Philip shook his head, backing up to the lane. "Don't you guys feel it? The air is cold..."

"Oh no! No way, no how, not again," Zach said. "Let's get Dad!"

It was almost as if their intention to leave the site calmed whatever was in the RV. With a last groan the camper righted itself and became still.

"Let's go," Chucky whispered.

"I'm gone." Zach's lunge to the lane kicked dirt onto Philip's shoes.

Zach was way ahead of Philip and Chucky as they rounded a bend, the RV out of sight behind them. Chucky was outwardly upset, slapping his ball cap against a pudgy thigh and making whistling noises through his pursed lips.

"You think he's going to say something to your dad? What in the world can he say? Your dad won't believe us."

"I can hardly believe it, Chucky."

Chucky laughed nervously. "Yeah! You can believe it or not, but I know what I saw." He crammed the cap down on his head and turned its bill to the back. "Well, I don't really know, do I? But it sure looked—"

"Chucky!"

A girl stood in the lane a hundred yards from them, hands on her hips as if she'd been waiting there for a long time.

"Oh, great." He jammed his hands into his pockets and hollered, "Whaddayawant, Casey?"

But Casey didn't answer. She stood firmly, waiting for them to get to her. When they did, she looked at her brother. "You're supposed to help me in the stable, Chucky. Mom said. And what was Zach yelling about?"

"I didn't hear him yelling about anything. Did you?" Chucky asked Philip.

Philip shrugged.

Chucky didn't know what to do. Should he stalk off toward the stables and get Casey away from here? Or should he beg off stable work and hope she left before Mr. Baxter came down the lane with Zach? He remembered now. He'd promised his mom he'd give Casey a hand with the mucking out today, even though he was not very comfortable around the horses. He couldn't back out of a promise to his mom.

"I do have to help Casey clean horse stalls," he told Philip.

It was too late. Chucky could see Zach towing his father along at a fast trot toward them.

"Philip?" Mr. Baxter came to a stop in front of them and tilted his head to one side, waiting.

"Tell him," Zach said. "Tell him how the RV was rocking in place, like there was an earthquake or something."

"Come on, Casey," Chucky said, trying to pull his sister along.

"What earthquake?" Casey tried to get her arm out of Chucky's grasp.

"It wasn't an earthquake," Philip said. "But it did look like something was rocking the camper, Dad, and we haven't seen Mr. Creach around."

Mr. Baxter sighed and seemed to be considering what should be done while Chucky kept trying to pull Casey away.

Zach scuffed his toe on the ground. "Dad, please. You gotta come check it out."

"Oh, all right," his father said, and started down the lane.

Chucky groaned when Casey set off behind him, then grinned when Mr. Baxter called over his shoulder to her. "Casey, go on back and tell your mom to keep an eye on the store for me. I'll be back in a minute."

"I'll be back in a minute, too," Chucky told her.

Philip strode alongside his father, listening to all the thoughts in his head crash into each other. What would happen when they approached the site? Would the RV go through its crazy dance again? And if it did, would his dad stand there in shock, feeling the cold swirl of air? Maybe Zach shouldn't have gotten Dad to come out here. What if nothing happened and his father thought they were making it all up?

"The car isn't here," Mr. Baxter said as they reached the site, and for the first time Philip realized that Mr. Creach's car was indeed gone. "But everything looks just fine," Mr. Baxter continued. "He registered for two weeks. He's probably sight-seeing."

"Does it look fine, Dad?" Zach asked. "Where's the ashes from campfires? Where's the cooler, or the rope clothesline? Where's the lawn chair, or the lantern?"

Mr. Baxter's gaze had been going from the fire pit to the picnic table, to the trees around the site as Zach asked his questions. Then it landed on the RV and Mr. Baxter went forward, arm outstretched to knock on the door.

Philip held his breath and noticed the others did the same.

RAP-RAP-RAP! "Is anyone in there?" their dad called out, his face close to the metal door.

The boys closed rank on each other. Zach felt a reassuring clammy shoulder on each side. He tensed along with the others as his father's hand gripped the door handle and turned it.

"It's open," Mr. Baxter said. If he thought it odd that the three boys were standing together like the three remaining pickets of a fence blown away in a storm, he didn't let on. "I'm going in," he said, making Philip think of the medical drama he'd seen last week where all the surgeons had used the same line.

"Aw man, aw man," Zach whispered like a chant.

The broad shoulders of Mr. Baxter stooped, then disappeared inside the RV. The boys stood tense and silent, not daring to take their eyes from the doorway. After a moment Mr. Baxter stepped out, jumping from the doorway to the ground. Keys jangled in his fingers and he waved a piece of paper at them.

Philip broke rank and ran to his father. "What is it?"

"Have a look," his father said and handed him the paper. "It beats me."

Philip held the paper between his hands and read it aloud as Chucky and Zach came up on either side of him. There were only three words on the paper, written in a large scrawl and underlined several times. It said:

KEEP THE CAMPER!!!

"I guess camping wasn't his cup of tea," Mr. Baxter said. "He's paid up, so this can sit here a while. But I'm not sure I can legally do anything permanent with it on the basis of a note. It isn't even signed."

"We'll lock it for you, Dad. You'd better get to the store." Philip didn't know why it was so important that he get to see inside the RV. It just was.

"I'd just as soon do it myself. I don't know what caused it to rock the way Zach described it. It could be unsteady." He inserted the key.

"Maybe we shouldn't lock it at all," Chucky said quickly.

Mr. Baxter looked at him through narrowed eyes and Chucky felt his face go hot. "I mean, what if Mr. Creach changes his mind and comes back, maybe in the middle of the night! He couldn't get in and he'd have to sleep in the car."

Philip shot an admiring glance Chucky's way.

"Okay," Mr. Baxter said. "Nobody's bothered it yet." He took one of the keys from the ring and handed it to Philip. "Toss this in on the table. I'll take the other one to the office."

"Okay, Dad. We'll be up in a while, after we walk Chucky to the stables." He slid Mr. Creach's note into his father's shirt pocket, then turned like he was going to put the other key in the RV.

They watched Mr. Baxter break into a brisk walk up the lane. Philip touched the handle on the door, and turned it slowly, then swung the door open.

"Dad doesn't believe me," Zach said.

"I think he does," Philip said. "He told us it wasn't safe, didn't he?" He poked his head inside. Then, with a deep breath he climbed up and into the RV.

Dust motes sparkled in a ribbon of sunlight that stabbed the humid atmosphere inside the camper. The RV tilted slightly as the other two climbed on board.

"Phew! Open a window," Zach said.

A tiny something crossed the back of Philip's neck and caused a bead of cold sweat to break loose from his hairline. For an endless moment nothing in the RV moved except for the bead of sweat. No one breathed; the dust hung still in the spear of light, and all the while the bead of sweat ran slowly down the right side of Philip's face. When it dropped from his jaw line everything exploded.

The built-in cabinets of the tiny kitchen area began to slam open and shut. The floor beneath their feet trembled and rolled. Arms flew as the boys tried to grab each other for support. Philip's eyes seemed frozen open as he focused on the cabinet below the sink. With each opening of the doors a toy car or truck flew out and hit the bench opposite.

He couldn't take his eyes from what was happening to see if the other two were seeing the same thing, but Philip felt their fear and the fingers that bit into his arms.

"Stop it!" Philip yelled the two words over and over and even in his confusion and terror, Philip could remember another voice yelling those same words.

"Let's go," he was suddenly able to say. Just as before the RV became quiet. The floor stopped its rolling and the cabinets stopped their slamming. It seemed they all took a deep breath together. "Let's go, now," he repeated.

One lone car, a red one, pointed itself at Philip's foot and rolled slowly toward him.

Chapter Four
Calling on the Corporal

As the toy car bumped Philip's foot, a shiver ran up his leg. The car coasted backward and Philip felt the cool air drift away with it. All three boys stood for a moment, dumbfounded. Then Philip spoke, his whispered voice cracking. "We've got to talk to Jared."

Chucky nodded, his eyes wide.

Philip noticed that Zach was shaking. Chill bumps covered his arms and his teeth chattered. "Come on, Zach," he said, taking his brother's arm.

Chucky followed as Philip guided Zach out the door. Philip swallowed the lump of fear lodged in his throat. *Someone has to be brave,* he told himself. Then, out loud he told them, "Jared will know what to do."

He was in the habit of taking charge, and that is just what Philip did. After checking to make sure the camper door was closed tight, he took off. Zach and Chucky followed.

As they moved down the winding path past the campsites, Chucky clamped his hands over his pockets to stop the jangle of junk inside. They made fun of him for carrying so many "goodies" but Chucky didn't care, because he was the one they turned to when they needed something, and he often had it, right there in the mess of junk they teased him about.

No one spoke for a while. There was no need to. They knew where Philip was leading them. They passed a campsite with two tents standing side by side. One was a large nylon tent with its window covers rolled up to catch the breeze. Beside it stood a screened tent with a picnic table inside it, a way to eat and keep the bugs off. There were pots and pans and a large cooler that sat in the middle of it all. A rope clothesline stretched between two leaning pines. It sagged under the weight of several wet towels. *That's what a campsite should look like,* Philip thought.

Every now and again as they walked, Philip heard Zach murmur, "Aw man, aw man, aw man," so he picked up his step. He was certain Jared would know what to do.

They moved quickly and soon they reached the spot behind the camp store where they had planted their garden before school ended. Philip came to an abrupt stop, and Chucky, who was deep in thought, almost ran right into him.

Philip plopped down on the stump on the edge of the garden plot. "Are you here?" he softly asked.

The other two sat down near him, waiting for an answer. Zach looked dazed, and rubbed his arms as if he were still cold.

"Are you here?" Philip asked again, and stared into the garden. He was remembering how Chucky had decided to plant flowers around the very same stump he was sitting on. And how he had dug up a metal piece that turned out to be the I.D. tag of a Union soldier from Civil War days. It was the I.D. tag of Jared Scott.

"Hey, Corporal Scott," Chucky said softly. "If you're here, we really need to talk to you."

Philip felt the cool air settle around them even before Corporal Jared Scott began to materialize. As he watched the ghost soldier form in a fog, take shape and become more solid, he smiled, remembering how scared they had been that very first time. His smile faded though, when he thought about the RV and the chilling reason they needed to talk to their friend.

"Jared," Zach yelled hopelessly, throwing himself at the ghost, flinging his arms around his waist. But his arms passed through Jared and he nearly fell over. His face reddened as he straightened. "I'm sorry, Jared. I'm so glad to see you. We need you."

Philip rolled his eyes. "Sit down and chill out," he told his brother, then turned to Jared. "We have a problem, Corporal. I hope you can help us."

Jared listened quietly, nodding from time to time as Philip and Chucky and Zach all tried to tell the story at once. They told about the cold air, and how the camper rocked and rolled. They ended with the toy car that had hit Philip in the foot and rolled away. Somehow he heard it all.

"So do you think it's a ghost? Do you think it can hurt us? Do you think it's evil...or what?" Zach was breathless and the chill bumps were still on his arms. He ended with a sigh through pursed lips, blowing his blonde bangs skyward.

Philip's hand settled on Zach's shoulder to calm him.

Zach nearly jumped a foot. "Don't do that," he hollered.

Chucky couldn't help but smile.

"Chucky Coppersmith! I'm telling!"

Chucky's smile faded. Casey stood behind him, her stringy hair sticking out from under one of Chucky's old ball caps. Her hands were on her hips. Chucky wondered whatever kept her hands from sticking there for good, since they were on her hips so often.

"You're supposed to be helping me in the stable again. I've done all but one stall and if you don't do the last stall you're gonna be in big trouble. I mean it!"

"Don't be so bossy," Chucky said. "You're gonna be in big trouble too, if you don't take off my hat!"

"Make me!" Casey said angrily. "Or maybe you can get your pretend ghost friend to take it off me," she said. "Isn't that who you're talking to?"

"Maybe he will," Chucky said, looking at the corporal.

The corporal stretched a hand over Casey's head as if he would do just that. It hovered there for a few seconds, and he wiggled his fingers. Then he smiled and stepped away. Chucky grinned.

"Now what's so funny?" Casey asked, glancing nervously behind her. She pushed a hand across her sweaty brow, then stomped off toward the stables. "Come on!"

"I guess I gotta go to work before she does tell Mom," he said sourly. "Let me know what happens." Chucky looked at Jared, marveling again at how Casey couldn't see him.

"Thanks for coming, Corporal," he said, saluting awkwardly, then stalked off after his sister.

Zach stood up and began to pace. "So what do you think, Jared? Are we safe or should we worry? Will you check it out?"

"Finally a good idea," Philip said. "Sit down, Zach." He pushed his glasses up on his nose and turned to the corporal. "Will you check out Mr. Creach's RV?"

Jared smiled, an amused expression crossing his face. His shaggy eyebrows arched into a question. "Shall I go alone?"

"Yes!" Zach said.

"No," Philip said, and Jared smiled again.

Jared smoothed the wrinkles in his blue uniform and straightened his cap. "Point me in the right direction."

The camper was quiet. Shut tight, it stood a lonely vigil in the section of the woods that Mr. Creach had requested, away from the other sites.

"This is the one?" Jared asked, puzzled. "Everything appears to be in order."

"Well, just wait until you go inside," Zach mumbled from behind Jared's back. "Just wait until you see how that joint rocks. I thought it was going to roll over on us!"

"It wasn't that bad, Zach."

Zach shot Philip an exasperated look. "You were scared too," he said. "Don't tell me you weren't."

"Let's go inside," Philip said, "so Jared can check it out."

"You aren't gonna go inside again, are you, Philip?"

"Well…"

"Why don't you stay here with me?"

Corporal Scott looked from one boy to the other. "Zach, stay here and wait. Philip, you show me inside."

Philip nodded grimly and motioned for Jared to go first. He followed the tall, broad shoulders of the corporal up the rickety steps, swallowing hard. Philip thought that if he weren't safe with Jared, there was no way he'd ever be safe.

Jared's body seemed to melt right through the camper door. Philip sighed, grabbed the door handle, opened it in the usual way, and stepped inside.

It took a moment for his eyes to adjust to the light, and to find Jared, who stood quietly near the kitchenette. The same shard of light as before came through the windowpane, but at a lower angle, piercing Jared, who seemed more transparent than ever. Dust motes floated through his kneecaps. Instead of being humid though, the RV was now cold. Very cold.

Philip wrapped his arms around his tee shirt and looked about. Not a toy car was in sight. He tried to read the corporal's face.

Jared reached out, palms up, to feel the flow of cool air. He turned, then his eyes focused on something in the corner and he smiled.

Philip held his breath, waiting.

At last Jared spoke, his voice a low, hollow rumble. "Oh my. I wasn't expecting a whippersnapper!"

Chapter Five
The Whippersnapper

Philip caught his breath at Jared's words. He felt a strange mingling of fear and relief that Jared had confirmed the presence of something inside the camper. He was about to ask Jared to repeat his words when a hard rapping hit the door. Philip jumped, his arm flying out and his hand swishing through the corporal.

"Philip!" Zach called from outside. "Dad's coming!"

Philip looked with wild eyes to Jared, who calmly motioned toward the door. "Go on," he said. "I'll catch up with you later."

Philip exited the camper, shutting Jared in with whatever it was, then ran to join his brother who paced at the edge of the lane. "Where's Dad?" he asked.

"He's in the truck," Zach explained, sweeping a wide arc with his arm. "He's going to be coming around this way any second. We gotta get out of here!" He grabbed Philip's arm and hauled him to the lane.

"He's just doing his rounds, Zach. We are allowed to walk around you know."

"Yeah, well," he huffed as they walked at an easier pace. "I didn't want him stopping to check his site log when you and Jared came busting out of there. And what did Jared say anyway?"

Philip shivered. "There is something in there. Jared could see it."

"No! Did you?"

"No. I didn't have time to before you banged on the door."

"It's another ghost, isn't it? Oh, I know it's another ghost." Zach chewed his thumbnail.

"Jared didn't use the word ghost. He said it was a whippersnapper."

Just then, hearing the truck behind them, they stepped to the side of the road to let their father pass. But he brought the truck to an easy stop.

"What are you two up to?"

"Just walking," Zach answered him. "Is everything where it should be, Dad? Any unregistered guests?"

Zach hoped his dad didn't hear the nervous ripple in his voice.

"None that I saw. Do you know of any?"

Oh boy, do I! he thought. "Nope!"

Mr. Baxter smiled at them. "I've got one area to check yet. Do you want a lift to the house?"

"Thanks, Dad. But we're going to meet Chucky."

Mr. Baxter nodded and pulled away from them. When he was out of sight around a bend, Zach tugged on Philip's arm.

"What did Jared say? A *what* snapper?"

"Whippersnapper," Philip repeated. "Whatever the heck that is."

Zach's eyes grew round. "That sounds bad, really bad! A whippersnapper...gosh!"

"Should we go back and wait for Jared?" Philip asked.

"Heck no. I'm not getting near that RV with that thing inside. I'm not getting snapped!"

* * * * *

"Where were you this afternoon?" Zach asked Chucky.

It was after dinner and Philip and Zach were lying at the edge of the garden when Chucky came around the camp store toward them.

"Mucking the stall wasn't enough for Casey," Chucky griped. "I had to help her take the saddles into the tack room, and since I was there she said I might as well help clean them, too."

He groaned as he sat gingerly beside Philip.

"What happened to you?"

"Did either one of you ever fall on a saddle horn?"

Philip and Zach laughed. "Guess I don't want to, huh?" Zach asked. He rolled to his side, rising up on an elbow.

Chucky laughed a little too. "The best part was when Casey tripped over my legs after I fell, and she landed on her butt!" His face grew serious. "But anyway, what did Corporal Scott say?"

Zach sat up. "It was terrible—"

"Zach, hold it...," Philip tried to interrupt.

"Awful, just awful, Chucky!"

"What is it, Zach?"

"It's a whipsnapper!"

"Whippersnapper," Philip corrected him.

"Whatever," Zach said to Philip. Then he looked at Chucky. "Doesn't it sound awful?"

"But what is a whippersnapper?" Chucky hoped one of them would be able to tell him.

"It must whip or snap at you," Zach reasoned.

Chucky looked confused. "Why didn't the corporal tell you what it was?"

Philip sat up. "Because we haven't seen him to ask." He explained to Chucky how he'd had to leave the camper just as Jared discovered the cause of its problems. "He said he'd catch up with us later. So we're going to wait here."

Zach lowered his voice. "I hope he's all right. He's been gone for hours."

Philip snorted. "What can happen to a ghost?"

Zach thought about it, then nodded. "I guess you're right."

"Did you call him?"

"A zillion times," Zach said. "If he doesn't come soon, I'm going in to get more dessert. I'm still hungry."

"What's new?" Chucky mumbled from the other side of Philip.

"What did you say?" Zach asked.

"I said, me too."

Philip hid a smile with the back of his hand and felt a light breeze on his neck.

"Hello, boys."

The voice came from behind them and they all scrambled to their feet, turning to see an amused Jared Scott.

"I'm only a corporal. You don't need to come to attention like that for me. Sorry I kept you waiting so long. And I'm sorry you rushed your dinner on my account, Zach."

"Aw man," Zach said, embarrassed.

"Can you please tell us what's in the RV?"

"I could, Philip. But I'd much rather you see it for yourselves. Could you come down there?"

"Yes," Philip said.

"No," Zach said. "If we keep running down there Dad is sure to see us again."

"Wait a minute, guys!" Chucky knew the debate could run for a while if he didn't step in. "Why don't we go later, when no one would see us?"

"In the dark?" Zach laced his fingers together and held his hands under his chin. "Jared, are you sure you can't tell us, huh?"

Jared chuckled softly. "It's more afraid of you than you are of it."

"That's what they say about snakes," Zach said.

Philip cleared his throat. "Chucky and I will meet you there at nine-thirty," he said to Jared. "If Zach wants to come, he can."

Zach sighed in frustration. "I'll be there."

* * * * *

They saw the soft blue glow of Jared Scott by the RV. Philip smiled and doused the flashlight as he thought of what Zach called the glow: Jared's nightgown. Together, the boys trotted up to meet Jared. Hastily, Philip checked the windows of the RV for a similar glow. There was none.

"Dad and Gloria think we're up on the hill," he whispered.

"Yeah," said a nervous Zach. "We're watching for satellites that Philip swears you can see if you look hard enough."

"Well, you can," Philip said. "Just because you can't sit still long enough to—"

"Guys," Chucky warned.

"Sorry," Philip replied. "Okay, Jared. Let's go."

With a nod Jared went up the stairs and melted through the door, taking the glow with him.

"It gives me the creeps when he does that," Zach said.

"Shhh," Philip breathed as he opened the door.

Jared's "nightgown" filled the camper with a bluish light. Each time he saw it, Philip recalled the night Jared had come into their bedroom in search of his I.D. tag. Then, it had terrified him. Now, it made him feel protected.

"You can come out," Jared said as Chucky shut the door behind him. "They won't hurt you. These are the boys I told you about."

Philip tightly gripped the cool metal barrel of the flashlight in his hand as the far edges of Jared's glow wavered. Their ghost friend held out a hand for something they could not see, and urged it to come closer.

"Aw man," Zach whispered, and glued himself to Philip.

"That's right," Jared said in soothing tones. "Show yourself."

The three boys watched in wonder as a white glow appeared at the far wall of the camper and meshed with Jared's blue, turning it milky.

"See his innocence?"

Jared's question wiped away all fear from Philip's being. Excited, he watched as a small form took shape, its hand in the big, safe one of the soldier. *The white glow is innocence,* Philip thought.

"Well, for goodness sakes!" Zach blurted. "It's just a little kid!"

"He's only five," Jared said.

Philip and Chucky were smiling at the young ghost, but Zach laughed right out loud. "Is that what you were afraid of, Philip?"

Just then, the milkiness surrounding the little boy wavered and rolled like a thundercloud. A cushion from the kitchen bench flew across the room, catching Zach on the forehead. Jared laughed quietly.

Zach looked at Philip and Chucky in surprise. "Well, I'll be snapped!" he said.

Chapter Six
Sam

Zach picked up the cushion and tossed it back onto the kitchen bench. He laughed nervously, not sure if he should be amused or afraid.

"Sam," Jared said sternly and the thundercloud became a being again, a small boy with blonde curls framing an innocent face. He was whitened by an outline of light, but his eyes were downcast.

"I'm sorry," he said, scuffing the toe of his sandal on the linoleum floor. His voice was soft and quivery and it floated on the air like a faraway echo.

Jared placed his hands on the young boy's shoulders.

Philip stared at the milky blue light that emanated from the point where ghost met ghost.

"Sam has been in this camper since the day his parents left him here." Jared rubbed the boy's arms and Sam looked up, his eyes going from face to face, searching. "He says he is waiting for them to come for him."

The pain that etched Sam's face brought tears to Zach's eyes. He wiped a hand across his brow and tried to smile at the boy.

"They told me to stay here and wait for them," Sam said. A small fluorescent tear on the edge of an eyelash sparkled like a ghostly diamond, then rolled down his cheek. "And I will." He sighed. "No matter how long it takes."

Zach drew in a ragged breath. "Where are they?" he asked quietly.

The boy lowered his head again. "They never came back."

Philip looked puzzled. "Where did you see them last?"

Sam's face darkened. "Mom told me not to ride in the camper." Then his face brightened. "But Dad said I could. He said it would be all right." He scuffed the edge of a brown sandal against the floor again, remembering. "Boy, was Mom mad!"

Zach let out a long sigh through pursed lips, making his bangs fly clear of his forehead. Chucky jiggled the junk in his pockets.

Philip was still puzzled. "What happened then?"

Sam covered his face and sighed. Suddenly his light began to fade. For a few moments he wavered between showing himself and disappearing, the light coming and going in shaky spurts of being. Jared ran a hand down the boy's arm in a reassuring gesture, and the arm turned pale blue, as if a light had come on inside. Philip gasped. Beside him Zach and Chucky did the same.

"What happened?" Zach pressed, feeling an urgency he didn't understand. A chill breeze crept over him. He felt it in his hair, and then it raced down his spine and up again. As he watched, the boy turned from white to pale blue...then white again. His form was as unpredictable as the clouds that rolled across the sky on a stormy day.

Zach felt the chill again. *He's only a little kid,* he told himself. Then he asked, "What happened when they left you in the camper?"

KABOOM! The sound was deafening, and the jolt that accompanied it knocked all three boys off their feet. They landed on their bottoms. Philip looked up just in time to see Jared and the child disappear. He swung the flashlight to look, but in an instant, the light went dead. As he tried the switch again, a mournful wail rang out.

Chill bumps rose over Philip's knees and ran down his legs. His hands were shaking as his mind raced. The flashlight was dead. He could feel Chucky and Zach beside him scrambling to get up, but the floor of the camper began to roll, the RV rocking from side to side. Even in his panic, Philip could picture the small boy rocking in agony.

"Philip!" Zach's voice was filled with terror. "Do something, Philip!"

Philip felt Chucky's hand on his arm.

"Let's get out of here," Chucky whispered, and the rocking stopped.

A heavy curtain of silence fell over them.

"Jared," Philip whispered.

"Jared," Zach repeated, his panic-stricken voice rising. But there was no answer.

In the darkness of the camper, Philip could feel Zach's rigid arm beside his own. He reached out and ran his hand down the cool arm until he could grasp his younger brother's hand. With Chucky leading the way, they felt their way to the camper door, Philip tugging a numb Zach along.

It was Chucky who found the outline of the door with his hand, located the door handle, and threw the door wide. He burst out of the camper with the other two on his tail. Chucky felt his feet slip on the wobbly metal steps, then all three boys tumbled down the stairs, landing in a heap on the ground. Philip and Chucky sat a moment, dazed, but Zach took off at a fast crawl, across the dusty camp path and toward the bushes. "Take cover," he told them in a loud whisper.

Moonlight spilled across Zach and the rest of the campsite. After the blackness of the camper the moon seemed as bright as morning sun to Philip, who picked himself up and dusted off his pants before following Zach.

Chucky rose in a jangle, his hands flying to cover his pockets and quell the sound.

The three of them stood in the shadows and stared at the camper. It was quiet and still, looking as normal as every other RV on the campground.

Philip could feel his heart racing. His knees were like jelly and his legs wobbled. For the first time in a long time, his mind was blank. He didn't know what to think. He couldn't make any sense of it. How could a tiny, innocent looking boy like Sam make all that happen? And why?

Chapter Seven

Creach Returns

The day was turning into a scorcher and it wasn't even noon. Philip, Zach, and Chucky weeded the garden, their minds on meeting Sam the night before.

"Anyway," Philip said, "until we see Jared again I don't think we can do much." He worked around the tomato plants, taking note of how small green tomatoes decorated each one.

"Maybe Jared is babysitting Sam."

"Ghosts don't need babysitting," Philip told Zach.

"Sam might." Zach tossed a handful of weeds to the lawn. "He's sad and afraid."

Philip hadn't thought of Sam as afraid, but he kept his mouth shut. He remembered the way he alone had felt Jared's frustration and sadness when they'd first encountered the soldier spirit. Something in Jared had touched him inside. Philip watched his brother from the corner of his eye. Maybe Zach was the one being touched now.

"Hot, isn't it?"

The boys groaned and turned to see Casey standing at the edge of the garden. A fluffy blue towel with red loopy designs hung over her shoulder and she wore a two-piece pink polka-dot swimsuit.

"I'm going for a dip in the pool. But I can since my chores are all done. And that's strange, because there is only one of me to do it all. Counting your ghost, there are four of you."

"Yeah, yeah, yeah," Chucky grumbled.

Zach flung a clod of dirt her way. "Just don't drown or anything, pest."

Casey laughed. "I'll be thinking of you poor guys when I dive in that nice, cool water."

As she turned to leave Chucky stood and ran to the water hose. "You want cool water?" he shouted, and aimed a sharp stream of water at her back. Casey squealed and took off running.

"Come on, Chucky," Philip said when they were through laughing. But Chucky didn't move. He stood peering around the corner of the store, then dropped the hose.

"Hey, guys, Mr. Creach is here!"

Zach and Philip looked at each other and ran to Chucky. Mr. Creach's station wagon was parked in the store's lot.

"That's him all right," Zach said. "Do you think he's going to take Sam? I mean, is he going to take the camper?"

"Let's find out," Philip said.

Stepping into the air-conditioned store was wonderful. Philip wiped his brow, Zach blew air up under his bangs, and Chucky removed his Angels ball cap. They all looked at Mr. Creach who stood at the counter across from Mr. Baxter.

"Soda," Philip whispered. He led the way past Mr. Creach. He smiled at his father and opened the cooler door.

"I'll sign anything you want, or need, on top of this bill of sale," Mr. Creach was saying.

"That's all fine, Mr. Creach," Mr. Baxter said. "But that's not my problem. I'm not in the business of selling RVs here. The people who come here already have them, or they're tent people."

"Can I leave it sit here, then? I'll sell it, run the ads, whatever. But can it sit here? I'll pay lot rent."

Mr. Baxter sighed. "I don't know why you'd want that extra expense. And it's a fairly old camper."

"Look, I was fool enough to buy it. There ought to be more like me out there somewhere."

Mr. Baxter laughed and shook his head. "You are very persuasive, aren't you? But I can't do it. Why don't you check out some RV dealerships?"

Mr. Creach drew his lips in so far that Philip thought he would swallow them. He folded the bill of sale and jammed it into his shirt pocket. "I'll just junk it," he said. "I'll have it hauled and junked. It'll be gone tomorrow. Thank you."

Mr. Baxter offered his hand for a shake. "I'm sorry I couldn't help."

Mr. Creach started out of the store and Mr. Baxter turned to the boys.

"You want those sodas?" he asked.

Philip looked down at the can he held and didn't remember opening it. "Yeah. We'll owe you, okay?"

Without waiting for an answer he took off at a trot. Chucky and Zach followed.

In the parking lot, Mr. Creach was getting into his car. Zach reached the driver's side as the old man shut the door.

"Mr. Creach, can we talk?"

Philip thought Zach would ask where Mr. Creach had gotten the camper, because it might give them a clue to Sam's story. He was surprised when Zach took a different track altogether.

"Why do you want to junk the camper, Mr. Creach? It's a good camper, really."

The old man looked at Zach through narrowed eyes. "You're the boys who live here."

"That's right. I'm Zach, and this is my brother Philip, and that's Chucky. We, I mean all of us, think it's a good camper. You shouldn't junk it."

Philip got a butterfly in his stomach when Mr. Creach turned his eyes on him. He swallowed and nodded his agreement with Zach.

"Hi," Chucky squeaked.

Mr. Creach made a noise like a goat bleating. "Bah! You boys run along now."

"Wait!" Zach laid his free hand on the window of the car door. Soda sloshed from the can in his other hand. "Please, sir, we know what's wrong with the camper, and we can fix it. We'll fix it here, and then if you want to junk it later…"

"Whoa," Philip whispered, amazed at his brother.

"Triple whoa," Chucky agreed.

Voices called and laughed throughout the campground. Traffic droned and insects buzzed. But at the station wagon, no one moved for a long time.

Then Mr. Creach rubbed his face with a calloused hand and sighed. "Why don't you tell me what you think you know about the camper?"

Relieved, Zach stepped back from the car door. He was thinking, *What the heck, tell him.*

"First of all, we should say we're sorry, because we went in there when we didn't have your permission."

Mr. Creach looked them over. Philip felt his cheeks turn red, and nervously adjusted his glasses. Then Mr. Creach said, "Never mind that. Go on."

Zach grinned. "We know there's a little boy in there. His name is Sam and something happened to his parents after they told him to wait there for them."

As Zach talked, the other two boys moved closer to the car to hear his hushed words. He told the story as best he could, explaining Jared as "a friend of ours."

Mr. Creach's face remained calm. None of the boys could tell what he was thinking. When Zach was finished, they waited for him to speak.

"This friend of yours…, you say he can help fix it?"

"Yes, sir," Chucky piped up. "We think so."

"What kind of person does this sort of work?"

The boys looked at each other, not knowing how to answer that. Chucky turned his ball cap around a couple of times.

"Well," Zach drawled. "He's kind of an expert on this stuff."

* * * * *

Philip dove off the low board for the fourth time, reveling in the way he could slice through the water until his hands touched the bottom. This time, when he touched the slick floor of the pool, he thought it felt colder than it usually did. He opened his eyes. If he'd been on the surface he would have gasped.

Through the bubbles he saw Jared lying relaxed in the water. He rose alongside Philip, who broke the surface sputtering and choking. Chucky and Zach, who had been waiting their turn to dive, were yelling at him from the side of the pool and pointing to Jared.

Philip took his time swimming to the side, catching his breath and feeling foolish because Corporal Scott seemed to float along with no effort, grinning at him like a kid.

"Ha-ha!" Chucky laughed. "That was so cool!"

"You're not even wet," Zach said to the ghost.

Philip, a little embarrassed at being frightened like that, turned on the corporal. "We were calling you from the garden. Why didn't you come?"

"I was attending to something else. I came as soon as I could." He perched on the side of the pool between Chucky and Zach. "What is it you want?"

The business-like tone in Jared's voice made Philip feel worse. Why did he think Jared should come at their call like a genie from a bottle? It wasn't fair to spend eternity like that! He wiped water from his eyes.

"We've got news. The camper's owner knows about Sam. He wants our help."

"I've been thinking about it," the corporal said. "Sam is not clear about a lot of things, but I've been talking to some of the guys around here, and there are some who have tried things I've never tried."

Philip felt a shiver run across his neck. He knew what guys the soldier was talking about. "Like what things?"

"Like how to get information, go places. What the..." Jared stopped abruptly as two skinny legs moved into his space. He shot backwards a little.

"What's so secret? Eeeww, what was that?" Casey asked, brushing each of her legs with a hand.

Philip saw the goose bumps popping out as he watched. "Go on, Casey. We didn't bother you and your friends."

He was surprised to see Casey's bottom lip quiver. "They aren't my friends," she said pulling her blue towel tighter around herself. "They're just new kids that come for a day or two, a week if I'm lucky. Then they go away and I never see them again. Now get out of my way, Philly, or I'll jump on your head!"

Philip moved, but didn't get a chance to yell at her for calling him by that stupid nickname. She threw her towel back over her shoulder and dove into the water.

"What a pain," Chucky said.

"Give her a break," Zach told him, his eyes on Casey as she swam away. "That must be how Sam feels."

Chucky and Philip stared at Zach, while Jared smiled and seemed to want to pat his head.

Chapter Eight
Sam Sleeps Over

Zach hadn't planned to go to the camper. He had started down the camp lane on a walk, just to think. He was confused about what Corporal Scott had said. What kind of things had the fellows who the corporal knew actually tried? And what kind of things could help Sam with his problem?

Now, Zach found himself on the fringe of Mr. Creach's campsite, staring at the pea green camper. The sun was low in the sky, as he stood beneath the shadows of a great oak tree. Watching the camper, he wondered what Sam was doing inside. He wondered what he did each and every day, and how it felt to be so alone at such a young age.

As he watched, Zach's thoughts turned to the mom he had never known. She'd died when Philip was three. Zach, two at the time, only knew his mom by the stories he'd heard his dad tell. Zach knelt down and pulled up a long stem of grass. He slipped

beside him. Zach gripped the cool fingers in his own warm ones. He couldn't understand the sudden need to protect this young boy who had once scared the ever-loving wits out of him. But he needed to help him find peace and security, and send him home.

"Hi, Sam," he said softly.

Chucky grinned, and noticed that Philip seemed speechless. He thought that was sure a hot dog of a different color.

Jared Scott moved toward Sam, brushing the boy's hair from his eyes. The gentle move touched Philip, in the same way Jared had touched him when they'd first met. Jared knelt in front of Sam. "We're going to help you go home," Jared told the boy. "You'll have to wait a bit, but we will get you back to your mom and pop. I promise."

Sam gripped Zach's hand a little tighter. Searching, he looked into the corporal's eyes. Then he looked up at Zach. Zach's eyes met Sam's. Then Zach nodded. He put an arm around what should be Sam's shoulders. "The corporal never makes a promise he can't keep," he told Sam. "We'll get you home."

* * * * *

Philip could hear Zach thrashing about in his bed. He couldn't believe the change in his brother. This was the guy who didn't want to get near the RV. Now he couldn't sleep for thinking of the ghost inside. Philip flipped on the light and Zach sat up.

"What's the matter? Can't sleep?"

Zach shook his head.

"Me neither. Thinking about Sam?"

"I can't stop thinking about him, and how alone he must feel. Sometimes I feel lonely for Mom, and I don't even remember her. Does that sound dumb?"

Philip rubbed his jaw and squinted at the light. Without his glasses on Zach was a blur. "No. I feel that way, too, sometimes. You know, I can barely remember Mom myself."

"Well, if we feel that way, imagine how Sam must feel. His mom and dad were his whole life, and they were stolen from him, all at once."

Philip nodded and reached for his glasses, which were lying on the nightstand.

"It's so dark there. I wonder what he does at night?"

Philip was silent.

"Should we go check on him?"

"No, Zach. I think we would just scare him. He's been alone all this time. He'll be okay."

"At least before he had Mr. Creach."

Philip grinned. "I'm not sure that was any better than being alone."

Zach lay back down. "You're probably right." Then he grinned, too. "But I bet it was fun scaring the daylights out of him!"

Philip rested on his pillow. "You know, we really should try to get some sleep."

"Yeah." Zach snapped the lamp switch off and folded his hands beneath his head. He stared at the shadows in the corner of the room, remembering the time that Jared had materialized there and scared them so much they had run screaming into the hallway.

All at once, a glow in the same corner brought energy into the room. The light was white, lighter than Jared's had been. With it came a shuffling sound, almost like an animal. Zach sat up, his eyes straining to see in the shadows.

He could see Philip rise beside him. He'd heard it too, and this definitely did not feel like Jared!

"Philip?"

Before Philip could answer, the glow became a bright wash of white light. Suddenly Zach knew who it was.

"Sam," he whispered.

"Zach," he heard from the corner. Then the light took shape and he could see the tiny boy, his blonde hair plastered to his wet, tear-streaked face, blue eyes as bright as the day.

"I was scared," Sam said.

"How did you find me?" Zach asked, bewildered.

"I could feel your energy."

"Energy?" Philip was surprised that a live person could project energy too.

"It was easy, because I wanted you so bad...," the boy whispered. "And I needed you."

Sam glided across the room to Zach's side, and rolled onto the blankets. He threw his arms around Zach's neck. Zach felt the tingle of energy slide down his body like an electric shock, but it wasn't unpleasant. Through the cool touch of the young boy, Zach felt a certain warmth unlike anything he'd ever felt before. He put an arm around the ghost boy and pulled him close in his mind.

"It'll be all right," he said, and he knew in his heart that somehow it would be.

Chapter Nine
Casey Meets the Corporal

Zach didn't remember falling asleep. He only knew that having Sam with him had helped him relax enough so that he could sleep. The warm cool tingle where Sam had pressed close to him in slumber had been soothing. But he'd wakened with a jolt when he realized the tingle had stopped. Rising up on an elbow, Zach scanned the room, his morning eyes blurry from sleep.

Sam was sitting on the end of Philip's bed. The pair were chatting away.

"What does it feel like, being a ghost I mean?" Philip hadn't realized Zach was awake. He was being typically Philip: gathering data, digging up facts, looking for answers.

"Umm…" Sam scrunched up his face as he thought. He was wearing the same pair of faded shorts and tee shirt he'd worn when they met him.

He rubbed a fist under his bangs as he thought. Then his eyes lit up. "It feels like cotton candy," he said.

"Cotton candy?" Philip was surprised.

"Yeah, cotton candy. It's like I'm all soft and fluffy, and floaty and stuff."

"Does that feel good?"

"Umm." Sam crossed his legs and leaned back on a palm, wiggling his sandaled toes as he thought. "Mostly, yes. But sometimes I change. I get all wispy or something. I have trouble staying together. That's when I disappear." He sighed.

"Wow! Neato," Philip said with a grin. "I wish I could do that."

"It's not neato," Sam said, his lower lip puckering out. I can't help it when that happens. It happens whenever I get mad, or like when I was trying to get Mr. Creach to notice me. I'd get so angry, and I would rock the camper, but he wouldn't help me, and I got so…so…"

"Frustrated," Zach finished for him.

Sam's eyes darted to Zach. Then he rushed across the room and leaped onto the bed. "Zach! You're awake!"

Zach wished he could ruffle the boy's blonde hair. "Did you get frustrated?"

"Yep. Frustrarated. That's what it was."

"Were you frustrated when we asked you what happened when your mom and dad left you in the trailer?" Zach shuddered when he thought of the loud noise and how the camper had rocked and felt as if it was being tossed aside. He remembered the darkness that followed and the lonely wail Sam had released.

Sam looked puzzled. "No," he answered. "I wasn't frustrarated then." His eyes began to tear. "I was *showing* you what really happened."

All at once something clicked and both boys finally knew what had happened to Sam's mom and dad. Zach held a palm out and Sam put his palm down on top of it. "What hit the camper, Sam?"

"It was a truck," he said, blinking back the tears. "It was a big truck. It hit Mom and Dad, and the car first, then it rolled into the camper...and me. I was sitting at the table, looking out the window. I saw it coming, I saw it all, then I got hit in the head."

* * * * *

Chucky met Philip at the pool house.

"Zach's taking Sam back to the camper for a nap," Philip said. When Chucky's eyes widened,

Philip explained what had happened during the night, and how Sam had spent most of the morning with them.

"Look," Chucky said, pointing through the diamond-shaped holes in the chain link fence. "She's been sulking all morning. What a pain."

Philip peered through the fence. Casey was sitting on the edge of the pool, one foot dangling in the water, a floppy hat hiding her face. She was the only person in sight, except for a pool guard who was busy cleaning debris from the filter. "She looks lonely."

"Well, maybe she is," Chucky grumbled. "But she doesn't have to make it my problem."

"Maybe we should tell her about Jared."

"You're nuts," Chucky said. He leaned against the fence and kicked a stone. "I wish Zach would come on."

The words were barely out of his mouth when Zach came trudging up the hill, chatting away with the corporal, who strode along beside him.

Philip laughed. "One of these days he's going to get caught talking to Jared that way and Dad's going to check him into the loony bin!"

Chucky laughed along with him. "Come on, guys," he yelled. "Last one in is a crazy old egg!"

Zach pushed past Chucky and Philip as they entered the pool area. Chucky pushed back, grinning playfully. "Even if you beat me, you're the loony one," he laughed. "We all saw you over there talking to thin air!"

"Excuse me. I am not thin air."

At Jared's dignified reply all three boys broke into laughter again.

As they passed Casey, she got up and walked to a spot farther down the side of the pool away from them, where she sat again. "Talking to your ghost again?" she asked sarcastically.

"Yep," Chucky said. "He's right here with me."

"I'm not falling for that," she said. "You always want to make me look dumb." Casey lowered her head. "But I'd settle for a ghost friend, if it was a friend that stayed," she murmured so low that only Jared heard her.

"Boys," Jared said. "Tell her about me."

Philip's eyes widened. "You're kidding, right?"

"No. Tell her."

"Jared wants us to tell you that he's real," Zach said. He felt bad for Casey. Seeing Sam's loneliness had triggered something inside him.

"Sure he's real," Casey drawled. She adjusted the floppy sun hat on her head and moved the two big red tassels that decorated its brim in the front. "And pigs fly, too."

"No," Philip said in earnest. "It's true. He's standing right beside me."

Chucky leaned in as Jared spoke.

"Did he just say something? What did he say?" No matter what Casey had said, the boys could tell she really wanted to believe them.

"He said you're a brat!"

"Chucky!" Zach elbowed his friend. "That's not what he said. He said he liked your hat. He said the tassels remind him of the hats that the Zouaves wore. But they didn't have brims, they were just little caps."

"It's called a fez, right Corporal?" Chucky was particular about what things were called if it had to do with soldiers.

Corporal Scott chuckled and nodded. "That's right, Chucky. Fezzes."

Casey's hand went to her hat. She stared at the space between the boys. Then she snorted. "Fez or not, I don't believe you."

"Well it's true, and he said it!" Philip insisted.

Casey jiggled her foot around in the water. "If he likes it, tell him he can have it."

Jared walked to the spot where Casey sat, and came to a stop right beside her. Now he leaned over and lifted the hat from her head.

Casey gasped and looked up, and watched the hat float up, up, up, stopping to hang in place about six feet off the ground.

Chucky, Zach, and Philip had watched the corporal as he lifted the hat from Casey's head and placed it on his own. At the same time, they had watched the expressions, which crossed her face.

First, Casey looked stunned. Her eyes were wide and fearful.

"He won't hurt you," Zach said. "Remember, he's our friend."

Then wonder filled her face, and she stood looking up at the hat, which floated just out of reach, until she stood up. "Wow! Your ghost *is* real!"

"Yep," Zach snorted. Then he began to giggle.

Philip's face was serious. "Casey," he said firmly. "You can't tell anyone. No one at all. It would put Jared in danger."

Casey's smile clouded over. "I know that. I'm not dumb!" She turned to gaze up at the hat and she smiled. "I won't ever tell, I promise."

Jared slipped the hat back onto Casey's head and turned to go. "I have to check on Sam," he told them.

"Is he leaving?" Casey asked, alarmed.

"Yeah, he never stays in one place for long," Chucky answered.

Then Jared spoke over his shoulder. "Tell her she has a friend now, one that's here to stay. Tell her I'll always be watching out for her."

Zach repeated the corporal's words to Casey. The smile on her face was one he thought that he'd remember for a lifetime.

Chapter Ten

The Ghost Ring

The jamboree was getting underway. Philip, Chucky, and Zach stood at the foot of the hill waiting for darkness to fall.

"Ditching Casey was harder than I thought," Chucky said. "It's a good thing Mom wanted help with the funnel cakes."

"She sure has been grinning a lot lately," Zach said.

"I hope she doesn't tell," said Philip. She hadn't told so far though, and that was a good sign.

A cool breeze lifted Zach's bangs. "Here comes Jared."

Jared, with Sam riding on his shoulders, materialized in front of them. "Good evening, boys. Are you ready to go?"

"Ready, sir!" Chucky snapped to attention and saluted.

"Don't call me *sir*," Corporal Scott said with a laugh. "There aren't any chicken guts on my arms." He strode past them, forging a path up the hill. The boys grinned, understanding the joke about chicken guts, which was what some of the soldiers called the golden braid that officers wore on their sleeves. Jared had once laughingly told them that he figured the braid would have blinded the enemy if only his commanding officer George Custer would have flapped his arms hard enough.

The country band was tuning up below the boys as they followed their ghost friends up the hill to the clearing on the top. Philip thought the soft glow was better than a flashlight and couldn't get over the fact that no one from the jamboree could see it.

Philip had no idea what Jared had planned; only that tonight Sam might find his way home. But home to what? To where? Jared had once been stuck here in Gettysburg because he died here. What if Sam found out he was to be stuck around the RV forever? Mr. Creach wouldn't be happy about that and he'd junk the camper. Sam could live for an eternity in a junk yard somewhere!

Philip glanced over to Zach who was concentrating on his feet. Was he thinking the same thoughts?

Zach was thinking that tonight he would have to say good-bye to Sam. He looked up to see Sam, astride Jared's shoulders, and quickly back down, feeling close to tears. He was happy for Sam, but he would miss him.

Chucky held his hands flat over his pockets to keep the jangling down. He just knew that whatever happened tonight on the hill would be triple-awesome, and he couldn't wait to get to it!

At the clearing, Jared lowered Sam from his shoulders and the three boys drew close. "What do we do?" Philip asked.

"It's like this," Jared said quietly. "There are those of us who have learned to use our form of energy. I have never attempted to go elsewhere. In fact, some of us can't go elsewhere. But there are those who can, and do. It is too complicated to go into, but just like in the physical world, our world has its own rules and possibilities. Some of us are learning all the time."

"Like today," Philip spoke up. "You picked Casey's hat right off her head. When we first met you, you couldn't hold your I.D. tag."

Jared smiled. "You're quite right. And that's what I'm talking about. Now, my friends and I have worked out a plan. It was devised by the more adventurous among us. I can not say for certain that it will work, but it seems to be our best chance. We are going to concentrate our energy to enable one of us to leave here and go, not to another place, but to Sam's parents. Will you help us? Or do you want to go?"

"We'll help," Chucky and Philip said.

Zach crossed to make contact with Sam's hand. "We'll help."

"That's fine." Jared smiled and winked at Chucky. "I think you are especially going to like this, Chucky. I'll call them and introduce you."

Philip wasn't sure he wanted to know more about Jared's "fellows" than he already did. He had assumed this was something they could do on their own, just the five of them. Zach looked a little unsure also, but Chucky looked ready to burst with excitement.

"Gather around, fellows," Jared called to the dark woods that surrounded them. "Come and meet the boys."

Philip froze. His heart beat a rapid tattoo. Afraid, anxious for whatever this experience would be like, he couldn't deny that he trusted Jared completely.

"Join rank," Jared said, and stretched out his right hand.

It happened so fast. A man appeared with his hand upon Jared's right hand. He smiled at the boys and stretched out his right hand, which was clutched by yet another man. In a dancelike motion the boys turned around where they stood and watched as a large circle of ghosts, all of them soldiers, formed around them.

Chucky looked into the craggy face of a Confederate soldier, only three feet across from him. The soldier didn't seem to see Chucky; he just stared off into the distance, as if he saw something Chucky did not.

Softly glowing in different hues of blue, gray, and white, there were men in dark, smart uniforms and others in mostly rags. Chucky picked out a sharp blue jacket trimmed in yellow and knew it was a Union cavalry soldier, just like Corporal Scott. He knew the one in the scarlet hat was from a Confederate artillery company. He could hardly believe that he was standing here, being surrounded by men he looked at in history books!

Zach, who was half-afraid to look up into the faces of the ghost soldiers, noticed the feet of them all. Some of them wore glistening boots, and there were a few who were barefooted. The ring of ghosts closed around them with its last member, who Zach was astonished to see, was a boy, not much older than himself. A drum jutted out from his waistline.

"Philip, Chucky, Zach. These are my friends. And fellows, these are the three boys you've heard me speak of. With them is little Sam, the one who needs our help."

Zach wanted to grip Sam's hand so tightly that he could feel his own fingers digging into his palm. He was aware that each man had died here.

Philip's body tingled with the combined energy of the circle of soldiers.

Chucky's eyes filled with tears that he hurried to brush away. These men fought each other, perhaps killed each other, and now they were holding hands! His complaints about Casey seemed unimportant and he promised not to be so smug anymore.

Philip spun around again, slowly this time, meeting each face with wide eyes. The self-lit circle held him, Chucky, Sam, and Zach like they were the hub of a wheel, and he realized that he wasn't afraid anymore.

"Sam," Jared said. "What are your parents' names?"

"My mom is Jean. Dad's name is Sam, too. Samuel J. Collins."

"Samuel J. and Jean Collins. Concentrate now, fellows," Jared directed.

The boys jumped when the drummer boy began a soft rhythmic beating on the drum. Philip was amazed when one of the soldiers, a man in ragged clothes, slung a rifle high on his shoulder and melted into the darkness. He left a gap that the two men on either side rapidly closed. Was the departing ghost one of the adventurous ones?

"Concentrate," Jared reminded them all. The boys turned their attention to repeating the names of Sam's parents over and over in their minds.

Sam whimpered, calling quietly for his mom and dad. Zach concentrated hard, holding close to Sam, not thinking about missing him any longer, only wanting him to be happy. Jared stood with his eyes closed, his face determined. Zach put more effort into it and closed his eyes too.

When it seemed that he couldn't concentrate any harder, Zach heard a voice. It was coming from somewhere above them, almost as if from the sky.

"Sammy? Sammy!"

Philip gasped and looked up. Sam looked up too, and yelled, "Mom! Mom!"

Zach felt Sam sweep away from him and he backed into Chucky. "Is she coming? Is his mom coming?"

"Yes, Zach. They're both coming," Chucky answered him.

Zach didn't open his eyes until he felt Sam's familiar tingly warmth surround his middle. Sam's smiling face made his heart surge.

"Oh, Zach! You promised me you'd help me, and you did. I won't ever forget you!"

"You be good, Sam."

"I will," he said softly. "Thank you, everybody!"

"Good-bye, Sam," Jared said.

A blue cloud settled down and around Sam, who became part of it. Philip could feel the love inside of it, could feel the happiness flooding through him. He slung an arm around Zach. Together the boys watched as the cloud began to fade.

Sam's voice came to them again, very faintly. "Good-bye."

"You okay, Zach?" Chucky asked.

"Heck, yeah," Zach said and cleared his throat. He spun in the circle. "Thank you, each of you."

There was a low rumble of men's voices as most of them said a few words to each other or answered Zach. Then they began to disappear, one after another.

Chucky was disappointed. He didn't want them all to go so fast. He spun around hoping to find one that would maybe linger a bit. He stopped when he came face to face with a Confederate officer. Chucky was embarrassed to realize he didn't recognize which rank the officer held. He wasn't as good at it as he thought.

"I'm sorry, Sir," Chucky stammered. He drew himself up straight and gave the man a respectful salute.

With a gentle smile the officer saluted back, his golden braid flashing in the moonlight. Chucky could swear he heard the soft brush of gloved fingers against a hat brim. The officer faded and Chucky dropped his salute, stunned.

"That was *incredible*!" Chucky yelled.

Jared laughed. "Wasn't it? I've never seen the likes."

The boys laughed, not knowing whether Jared was talking about the circle of spirits or the salute. Zach felt light and happy inside for the first time in days.

"How about joining us for a funnel cake, Jared?"

"Maybe I will, now that I can hold one!"

They laughed harder, all of them giddy from the experience they'd just had. Philip looked up at the sky, wondering if he'd ever experience anything like it again. "Hey!" he said. "There's a satellite."

"I meant to ask you about that," Jared said. "I heard you arguing about satellites, and I want to know what they are."

"I still don't believe you can see them," Zach said.

They were all peering up at the sky. "I see it, too," Chucky yelped.

Philip grinned. "Okay everybody, get on your backs. Lesson time. Jared, you've got a lot to catch up on!"

* * * * *

"I can't tell you how grateful I am." Mr. Creach shook each boy's hand, then reached into the station wagon and pulled out a brown grocery bag, which he handed to Philip. "I thought you'd like to keep these as a reminder, and a payment of sorts. It's the boy's cars from the camper. Oh, and I'm sorry your friend isn't here to thank."

"We'll tell him for you," Chucky said with a sideways glance at Jared, who grinned and doffed his hat at Mr. Creach.

Zach held his hand behind his back and grinned too, the paper between his fingers fluttering softly in the breeze.

"You do that." Mr. Creach got into his station wagon; his newly claimed camper hooked up to the tow hitch. "I'll be back next year."

"We'll be glad to see you," Philip said.

As the wagon started, Zach ran to the back of the camper to tape up the diamond-shaped sign he'd made from construction paper. The black letters on it said *NO GHOST ON BOARD!*

Zach shouted as the camper pulled away. He pointed to the sign and Philip and Chucky laughed. Jared ruffled the hair on their heads, one after the other, knocking Chucky's cap to the ground. "You bunch of whippersnappers! What are you going to get into next?"

Philip, Zach, and Chucky looked at each other. None of them knew the answer to that!

Fact-finders

Look for books about ghosts or the Civil War in your school and public libraries. For more information on the Battle of Gettysburg and the supposed ghosts that haunt that area, here are two places for you to contact.

Gettysburg National Military Park
97 Taneytown Road
Gettysburg, Pennsylvania 17325
(717) 334-1124

Or visit the National Park Service on the web at www.nps.gov and follow the links to the park of your choice.

Ghosts of Gettysburg
271 Baltimore Street
Gettysburg, Pennsylvania 17325
(717) 337-0445
www.ghostsofgettysburg.com

Call or write to find out how to order Mark Nesbitt's books or take a ghost tour of Gettysburg. Tell Mr. Nesbitt the Gettysburg Ghost Gang sent you!

If you'd like to see a Gettysburg Ghost Gang Club formed, send a postcard with your name and address to:

Gettysburg Ghost Gang
P.O. Box 70
Arendtsville, Pennsylvania 17303